And we all go travelling by, bye-bye,
And we all go travelling by.

I spy with my little eye,
You can hear with your little ear,

A bright red truck goes *rumble-rumble-rumble*.

A yellow school bus goes *beep-beep-beep*.

And we all go travelling by, bye-bye,
And we all go travelling by.

I spy with my little eye,
You can hear with your little ear,

A long blue train goes *chuff-chuff-chuff.*

A bright red truck goes *rumble-rumble-rumble.*

A yellow school bus goes *beep-beep-beep.*

And we all go travelling by, bye-bye,
And we all go travelling by.

**I spy with my little eye,
You can hear with your little ear,**

A shiny pink bike goes *ring-ring-ring.*

A long blue train goes *chuff-chuff-chuff.*

A bright red truck goes *rumble-rumble-rumble.*

A yellow school bus goes *beep-beep-beep.*

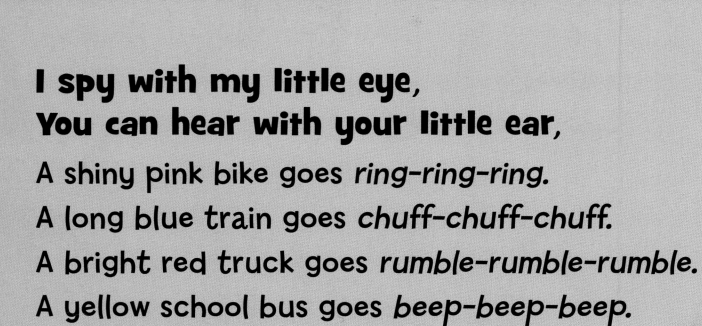

And we all go travelling by, bye-bye,
And we all go travelling by.

I spy with my little eye,
You can hear with your little ear,

A little green boat goes *chug-a-lug-a-lug.*

A shiny pink bike goes
ring-ring-ring.

A long blue train goes
chuff-chuff-chuff.

A bright red truck goes *rumble-rumble-rumble*.
A yellow school bus goes *beep-beep-beep*.
And we all go travelling by, bye-bye,
And we all go travelling by.

I spy with my little eye,
You can hear with your little ear,

A big white plane goes *neeeeeeee-oww.*

A little green boat goes
chug-a-lug-a-lug.

A shiny pink bike goes *ring-ring-ring.*
A long blue train goes *chuff-chuff-chuff.*
A bright red truck goes *rumble-rumble-rumble.*
A yellow school bus goes *beep-beep-beep.*
And we all go travelling by, **bye-bye**,
And we all go travelling by.

I spy with my little eye,
You can hear with your little ear,

A fast orange car goes
vroom-vroom-vroom.

A big white plane goes *neeeeeeee-oww*.

A little green boat goes *chug-a-lug-a-lug*.

A shiny pink bike goes *ring-ring-ring*.

A long blue train goes *chuff-chuff-chuff*.
A bright red truck goes *rumble-rumble-rumble*.
A yellow school bus goes *beep-beep-beep*.
And we all go travelling by, **bye-bye**,
And we all go travelling by.

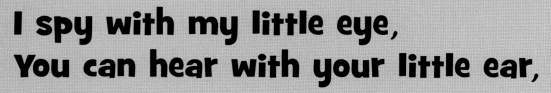

I spy with my little eye,
You can hear with your little ear,

Two purple shoes go *tap-tap-tap*.

A fast orange car goes *vroom-vroom-vroom*.

A big white plane goes *neeeeeeee-oww*.

A little green boat goes *chug-a-lug-a-lug*.
A shiny pink bike goes *ring-ring-ring*.
A long blue train goes *chuff-chuff-chuff*.
A bright red truck goes *rumble-rumble-rumble*.
A yellow school bus goes *beep-beep-beep*.

**And we all go travelling by, bye-bye,
And we all go travelling by.**

I spy with my little eye,
You can hear with your little ear,
A loud silver bell goes *ding-a-ling-a-ling.*

And we all start another school day, **hooray!**
And we all start another school day!

Travelling By!

A yellow school bus

A bright red truck

A long blue train

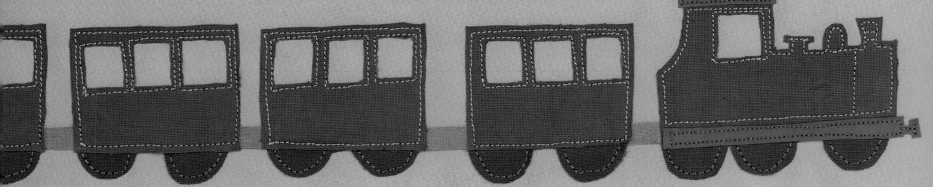

A big white plane

A shiny pink bike

A fast orange car

A little green boat

Two purple shoes

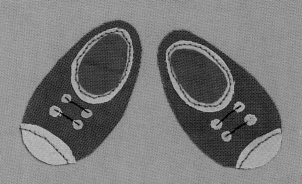

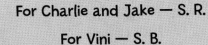

For Charlie and Jake — S. R.

For Vini — S. B.

Barefoot Books
29/30 Fitzroy Square
London, W1T 6LQ

Text and music copyright © 2003 by Sheena Roberts,
Playsongs Publications Limited, adapted from an original song,
'I spy with my little eye', copyright © 1995 by Sheena Roberts, Playsongs Publications Limited
Illustrations copyright © 2003 by Siobhan Bell
The moral rights of Sheena Roberts and Siobhan Bell have been asserted
Lead vocals by Fred Penner. Musical arrangements © 2003 by Fred Penner
Recorded, mixed and mastered by DaCapo Studios, Canada
Animation by Karrot Animation, London

First published in Great Britain by Barefoot Books, Ltd in 2003
This paperback edition first published in 2021

Graphic design by Barefoot Books, UK and Mayfly Design, Minneapolis, USA
Colour separation by B & P International, Hong Kong
Printed in China on 100% acid-free paper by Printplus, Ltd
This book was typeset in GrilledCheese and Billy
The illustrations were prepared using hand-dyed cotton sheets

Paperback with enhanced CD ISBN 978-1-84686-654-8
Paperback ISBN 978-1-64686-442-3

British Cataloguing-in-Publication Data: a catalogue record for this book is available from the British Library

1 3 5 7 9 8 6 4 2

Go to *www.barefootbooks.com/travellingby* to access
your audio singalong and video animation online.

I spy with my little eye,
You can hear with your little ear,
A yellow school bus goes *beep-beep-beep.*

We All Go Travelling By

BUS STOP

Written by **Sheena Roberts**   Illustrated by **Siobhan Bell**   Sung by **Fred Penner**